THE Return of the Big Bad Wolf

Liam Farrell

Illustrations: Terry Myler

THE CHILDREN'S PRESS

To
Róisín

First published 2004 by
The Children's Press
an imprint of Anvil Books
45 Palmerston Road, Dublin 6

2 4 6 8 7 5 3 1

© Text Liam Farrell
© Illustrations Terry Myler

ISBN 1 901737 48 9

Origination by Computertype Limited
Printed by Colour Books Limited

Contents

Wolf Haven

When you last heard from me, I had
been on trial for Causing Bodily Harm
to Mr Humpty Dumpty and Damage
to the houses of the Three Little Pigs.

Just for starters!

All lies, of course.

And what happened?

That old dope of a judge, Bill Boar,
bit the dust. My case was put back.

I would have to face a *retrial*.

A car was waiting outside the court. A long, long car. Shiny black. With a smart driver in a peaked cap.

'At your service, sir,' he said, bowing from the waist.

'Is this for me? Who owns it?' I asked as I got in. Anything to get away from those gaping crowds.

'You'll soon find out,' he smiled.

We drove deep into the forest and after a while came to a great gateway with pillars. It seemed to open by itself and we swept in. We stopped before a large house, all lit up. Steps led up to the front door.

'Welcome to Wolf Haven,' said the driver, opening the car door for me.

As I got out, the three wolves I had seen in court came down the steps to

greet me. My lawyers had told me that they were members of wwwdot (World Wide Wolves), the Wolf Rescue branch.

'You've had a hard time,' they smiled. 'But not to worry from now on. We're taking your case. With us behind you, you'll win the retrial.'

I was ushered in and shown to a lovely suite of rooms. When I had had a shower and put on the new suit laid out for me I felt like a new wolf.

Dinner was a meal to linger over
but the wolves ate so fast that it was
eaten in no time.

Maybe they wanted me to have an
early night so that I would be fresh to
talk to them about my case.

I had a few ideas for getting the
better of those Three Little Pigs.

But no. When the plates were cleared away, they set up a screen and a projector.

We were about to see a film!

What would it be? *Snarler 2*? *Lord of the Wolves*? Maybe an oldie. *Gone with the Wolves* or *My Fair Wolverine*.

I sank into a soft deep chair and relaxed. What a perfect end to what had been a dreadful day!

The Film

The lights were dimmed and the film began to run.

But what was this? Where were we? Then the penny dropped.

We were inside the court where I had spent so many awful days.

But who was this goopy-looking guy who looked like a nervous wreck? Couldn't sit still, never mind straight. Kept putting his hand to his mouth and rolling his eyes like he'd just heard he was about to be bitten by a snake.

Then he turned and looked straight at the camera.

I froze.

It looked just like me.

But it couldn't be me. Or could it?

I was really confused. My head was starting to swim and the screen was getting blurred. I hadn't taken my little red pills after dinner.

I heard the sound of low voices behind me.

'It's even worse than we thought.'

'Can't sit up straight.'

'Can't talk. Mumbles. Can't say two words without "Eh..." and "Ah..." and "You know...".'

'Why does he look so shifty? Like he's hiding something.'

'Any judge would convict him of anything.'

I was about to ask who they were talking about when Wolf One stood up, gave me a pat on the back and said with a smile (that is, if you can call a wolfish baring of the teeth a smile).

'Time for shut-eye. We have an early start in the morning.'

The First Day

The meaning of 'first thing' didn't hit me until the alarm went off next morning. I opened one eye.

Six o'clock. *Six o'clock!*

I put out a paw to switch it off but it wouldn't switch off.

It kept on ringing.

And ringing.

Next minute I was on the floor.

The bed had doubled up and thrown me out.

'Get up, you lazy swine,' snarled a loud-speaker on the wall. 'Be in the gym in two seconds flat.'

For a moment I was really mad. Who did they think they were?

Ordering ME around!

Then I thought again. They were going to help me in the retrial. Keep me out of prison.

Maybe this was an American idea: 'Rough 'em up and shake 'em out.'

Anyway, I couldn't leave. I had no clothes. They had all gone – except a skinny, pink sweat suit. Pink!

In the gym, a great, big, bruiser of a gorilla was waiting for me.

'What a nice day,' I said to him in a nervous voice.

'Not for you, chump,' the gorilla growled, hurling me to the ground.

'Press-ups. Come on. Look sharp.'

With a huge effort, I raised myself ten centimetres off the ground.

CALL THAT A PRESS – UP ?

'Call that a press-up? That's a cat laugh. Your muscles are jelly.'

He wrote down on a pad: 'Press-ups, zero. Zilch.'

It was the most horrible morning
of my life.

I had to run on a thread-mill until I
fell over in a heap.

Jump over spiked rails. Pull elastic
ropes apart. Stoop under low bars.

Climb bars to the ceiling.

Sit in a boat and row a hundred
strokes a minute.

And all the time this baboon, stop-watch in hand, was jeering at me, poking me every time I came within range and timing everything.

He wrote so many 'Zilches' he had to get a new pad.

At noon, a tray came in. Lunch.

As I sank into a chair, the cover was lifted.

'Lunch' was three leaves of lettuce. To be washed down with a gallon of water.

After lunch, the three wolves came in. I was stood against the wall.

'Can't stand up straight! His spine is crooked!' Wolf One looked cross. 'We'll soon cure that.'

So they strapped a pack with a load of very heavy bricks on to my back. I almost fell over backwards.

'Straighten up. Don't waddle. Tummy in. Chin in. Feel as if you had a ramrod up your spine.'

Wolf Two, a mean, ferrety-looking animal with a scowl, wasn't happy with me either.

'All these zeros,' he said in a whining voice, looking at the gorilla's pad. 'Can't you do *anything*?'

'I'm trying,' I said. 'But I feel a bit weak, because I've had nothing to eat. If I had a good meal....'

At least that's what I thought I said.
Wolf Three, a sour, dour-looking
nut, at once produced a tiny tape
recorder and pressed 'Play back'.

'I'm...eh... trying,' was what came
out. 'But...ah...I feel a bit weak...like
... because I've had nothing to eat...
you know...if I had a good meal... you
know like...I could do...eh... better.'
There was much shaking of heads.

'Can't speak,' said a parrot who was lurking in a corner. 'Just mumbles.'

'The rules of good speech,' said Wolf One, 'are: "Get up, speak up and shut up." Got it?'

'I'm here to teach you to speak,' said the parrot.

'And if I hear one more "eh" or "ah" or "you know" or "you know, like you know", I'll bite you.'

I'LL BITE YOU

'Start him with a...e...i...o...u,'
said Wolf Two

So I spent the whole afternoon
walking around with a ton of bricks on
my back, saying a...e...i...o...u until
I was hoarse.

This went on until six o'clock.

Then it was more lettuce and water
and an early night.

The Escape

I stuck it for three days.

Then I got a dreadful shock.

As I was passing the wolves' sitting room, I heard them talking.

'We must do something about his nose. It's not straight. Gives him a nasty, shifty look.'

'And his eyes are all wrong. Too round. No wonder he looks goopy.'

'Needs a new face, if you ask me!'

My blood ran cold. The thought that they wanted to give me a face-lift was the last straw.

I knew I could stand it no longer. Not for a day longer.

'Am I a wolf, or a mouse, to put up with this?' I thought. 'It's sheer hell. It's worse than jail. There, at least, you get food. And there are people to talk to.'

I waited until after 'lunch'. Then I had a big break. Wolf Two, he of the a...e...i...o...u's, was late.

I leapt at the only window in the gym. It was left open to ensure a supply of icy air. On the theory that I could never jump so high.

Well I got there on my first try, and dropped down on the other side. Then I legged it to the fence around Wolf Haven.

As ill-luck would have it, a lone wolf was loping around, rifle in hand.

I waited until he had passed, then rushed out and clocked him from behind.

He went down like a stone.

That baboon of a gorilla would have been pleased if he could have seen me in action.

The last three days had turned my muscles from jelly into iron.

Then I leaped over the outer fence (a cake-walk!) and just ran and ran and ran. I wanted to put serious space between me and Wolf Haven.

I only stopped because I caught my foot in a tree root and fell.

As I lay there, flat out, I began to feel safe. Why would wwwdot bother about me? From their point of view I was a dead loss. Bound to lose my case in court. They wouldn't even bother to look for me.

Still, I decided to hide out before the retrial. Just in case.

As I lay back, looking up at the sky
and the trees and the leaves, I
wondered where I was.

I didn't know this part of the forest.

Suddenly, I heard the sound of
singing. A high-pitched kind of
squeaking. A few voices. After a while
I could make out the words:

Here's to the health of the Big Bad Wolf,
  Big Bad Wolf, Big Bad Wolf,
Here's to the health of the Big Bad Wolf,
  He really got a raw deal!

The Three Little Pigs! Singing *my* health! Saying I had got a raw deal! What on earth was up?

I simply had to find out.

I ran towards the sound of the singing. As two of their houses had been blown down by the storm, I thought they must all be living in the stone house of the eldest pig.

But no! They had rebuilt all three
houses, even the stone one. And they
were simply HUGE.

Three storeys.

Glass from top to toe in one.

Columns straight out of the Old
South on the second.

A huge dome on the third.

All set in smooth green lawns.

The Three Little Pigs

On a patio at the back of the biggest house, a butler was serving drinks.

At last one of the three saw me.

'Well, if it isn't old wolfie. Come on a social call.'

'Sit down,' invited another. 'Here's a chair.'

'Have a glass of champers,' giggled the youngest.

I stared at them. I moved my mouth
but nothing came out.

'What's your problem?' asked the
eldest pig.

'It's that song - *Here's to the health of
the Big Bad Wolf.*'

'Well...it's a long story but I'll cut it
down to size. After the trial we acted
smart. Hired a PR hot-shot.'

'What's PR?'

'Public Relations. A smart guy. If you're in the news, he's your man.'

I was all at sea. 'What does he do?'

'Sells your story for you.'

'Tells you what to do, where to go, to get the top price.'

'How to talk to the press, TV, radio. Dressed us up in choir-boy collars. For the angelic look.'

'Said we must have three different stories. To cover all angles.'

'We've been on all the big shows.
*The Late Late, Live with Daniel, Tea
with the Porkies.*'

'He does all this for nothing? That's
very kind of him.'

'Boy, are you dim. Cost us an arm
and a leg. But it was worth it. Made
us millions.'

'You mean you haven't seen all the
headlines?' smirked the eldest pig.

How could I? I was in prison!

'Have a look,' chirped the giggler.
They held up papers. Great black
headlines, miles high, leaped at me:

'You blew it, wolfie,' said the eldest
pig sadly. 'Threw it all away. Nothing
to show for it, have you?'

'I was written about in *The Daily
Howl*,' I said, smarting.

They all fell about laughing.

'What did you get for that? Zilch!'
The eldest pig threw out an arm.
'Look at our houses! And take a peek
through the window.'

I peeked. And saw three massive
cars, each as long as a wet week-end.
'Jeeves,' shouted the middle pig.
'Bring in the caviare.'
'How do you like Jeeves?' asked the
eldest pig. 'He's from England. Used
to work for a Duke. Adds a touch of
class, doesn't he?...What are your
plans, by the way.'

No way was I going to tell them
about Wolf Haven and *that* saga.

'My case is being taken up by World
Wide Wolves,' I said.

'That lot?' said the middle pig.
'I'd watch my step there.'

'Yeah. Their plan is for you to lose
the case. Then they plan a huge drive
to say how wolves are the target for
racist abuse. You're no good to them
free. They want you behind bars.'

I couldn't believe my ears!

'But not to worry,' said the eldest pig. 'Your troubles are over. We talked it all over, the three of us.

'We thought how much we owed to you and what a raw deal you got.

'So we're going to make it up to you. At the next trial, we'll tell the judge that you *didn't* push Humpty Dumpty off the wall.'

39

I couldn't believe my ears (for the second time). Was this for real?

'But you'll go to jail,' I stuttered.
'Well, if that's how the cookie crumbles, so be it.'
'We'll take what comes,' said the middle pig bravely.
'Will prison be awful?' asked the youngest pig. His voice had a quaver in it and a tear shone in his eye.

I still couldn't get used to the idea
that the Three Little Pigs were going
to help me. I thought of all the nasty
things I had said about them.

'This is so good of you...' I began.

'Think nothing of it.' The eldest
pig took me by the arm and led me to
the door. 'Now, go and relax. Have a
real rest. A few good meals. All your
troubles are over.'

'Keep out of sight until the trial,'
called the middle pig. 'And don't go
near that lot in wwwdot again.'

I heard more singing as I left. Not the one toasting my health. This was a strange new one:

> *If I were a blackbird,*
> *I'd whistle and sing,*
> *I'd follow the ship*
> *That my true love is in...*

There was a thud as of something heavy falling and a sudden yelp.

The singing stopped all at once.

'We told you never to sing that song again,' hissed the eldest pig.

'Or say that word again,' added the middle pig.

Well, it was none of my business if the youngest pig (I was sure it was him) had got himself into trouble.

I went on my way, my heart full to overflowing.

Those dear little pigs. They had seen the error of their ways. They were about to tell the truth.

My good name would be cleared.

I would visit them every day in prison, I vowed.

'Pssst...' A hiss from the bushes brought me back to earth.

It was the butler.

'Can I have a word in your shell-like?' he said in a whisper.

'My what?'

'Your ear, idiot.'

He put a finger to his lips, then pointed a way through the bushes.

I followed him.

When we were in a small open space, he stopped.

'Only got a mo,' he said. 'Must get back to serve dinner. But I can't bear to see a nice old gent like you being set up.'

'By whom?' I asked. I decided to ignore the 'old'.

'By those three little crooks.' He pointed back towards the house.

Surely he didn't mean the Three Little Pigs?

'But they're going to help me.
They're going to tell the judge the
truth. That one of them pushed
Humpty Dumpty off the wall.'

'The truth? And you believe them?
They couldn't tell the truth to save
their bacon.'
Boy, was I confused?

'Then why did they tell me all that?'

'Lull you into doing nothing. Then they'll turn up in court and you'll be for the high jump.'

' But what am I to do?'

'*I* can't tell you...but I can give you a clue. I heard them say there was a missing witness. *Someone who had seen Humpty Dumpty being pushed.* And could prove it wasn't you.'

THERE'S A MISSING WITNESS !

'Who was it and who's the witness?'

'Haven't the foggiest. But anytime
anyone says the word "blackbird" they
go mad - two old older pigs that is.

'And when the young one sings
that song they throw things at
him...now I'll have to breeze – dinner
on the menu.'

He vanished and I was left alone in
the middle of the forest. No friends.
Enemies all around.

And nothing to go on but the word
'blackbird'.

The Castle

After a while walking, humming that stupid tune out loud, I came to a high wall and a gate with a coat of arms on it. It was the Palace!

At that moment, the gate flew open and a girl with her nose in bandages rushed out.

She pointed a finger at me.

'What do you mean by singing that stupid song?'

Suddenly it all came back to me:

The King was in his counting-house,
    Counting out his money.
The Queen was in the parlour,
    Eating bread and honey.
The Maid was in the garden,
    Hanging out the clothes,
When down came a blackbird
    And pecked off her nose.

I stared at her.

'You're the maid!' I said to her.

'Yes, I am. But I won't have people singing silly songs about me. Besides it isn't even true.'

'But everyone knows the blackbird pecked off your nose.'

'He did no such thing. That was just made up by the media to make a good head-line. You know how they are. As if I'd allow a dumb blackbird to peck off my nose.'

'But why the bandages?' I asked.

'Well, it was like this... The black-bird *did* scratch my nose and my lawyer said I should put in a Personal Injury Claim. So I did – I never liked my nose anyway. When this heals, I will look really beautiful.'

'When did this happen?' I asked.

'I'll never forget it...it was the day Humpty Dumpty fell off the wall. I had come out into the forest to pick some wild flowers and it all took place right in front of me.'

'What *did* happen?'

'I saw Mr Dumpty come out of his house and get up on his garden wall. He started shouting at someone and waving his walking stick but I couldn't hear clearly.

'Then I saw the eldest of the Three Little Pigs sneak up behind him and push him off the wall.'

'Did anyone see you?'

'No. When the row started I hid behind a bank. No one could have seen me.

'Then all the King's Horses and all the King's Men came by and took Mr Dumpty away.

'I crept away back to the Palace – we're not supposed to leave the grounds, you know.'

'Did you know I was on trial for pushing Humpty Dumpty?'

'I heard about it, later...you see, at the time I was just about to go into hospital to have my nose altered and my lawyer told me to lie low. That the claims people might ask questions. Say my injury was not serious, that it was a put-up job.

'When I got out the first trial was over. But I'll be here for the next.'

'And you'll tell the judge what you've just told me?'

'Of course? It's my duty as a citizen to do so.'

I didn't ask her why she didn't do her duty first time round.

Was I getting smart?

'Besides,' she went on, 'I can't stand those Three Little Pigs. They come up to the castle, put their dirty trotters up on the best satin chairs and order me around as if I were their servant.'

We parted and she said she would tell my sad story to the King and Queen and that maybe I would be invited to their next garden party.

'After all, they seem to invite every Tom, Dick and Harry, so there should be room for you.'

The Retrial

I *was* invited to the garden party and the King actually took me aside and he and the Queen spoke to me.

He, too, was getting fed up with the Three Little Pigs. They had put *By Royal Appointment* on their notepaper. And she was mad because their butler was dressed in purple and crimson, the royal livery.

'Where did they get *that* uniform?'
she asked. 'That I'd like to know.'

Then they told me the name of the
lawyer I should get.

'Kerry "Lockjaw" Blue – he's your
hound,' said the King.

'*Never lets go!*' said the Queen.

At the trial, it was a matter of
OUT, OUT, OUT!

Attack on Red Riding Hood's
Grandma – *no evidence.*

Knocking Humpty Dumpty off the
wall – *thrown out on the evidence of the
Castle maid.*

As to the charge that I had knocked
down the houses of the Three Little
Pigs, old 'Lockjaw' really went to
town on that one. He held up a
report from the *Village Weather Eye* to
prove that there was a Force Nine gale
blowing that day.

OUT! OUT! OUT!

'The first house,' he thundered,
waving an invoice in the air, 'was built
of *straw!* And do you know what was
holding it together?'

Pause to make sure everyone was
all ears. '*String. Cheap string!*'

Gasps all around.

'As for the second house? That was not much better. It was made of sticks. Sticks held together with inferior glue.

'Now for the stone house. I'm not surprised the roof came off. The slates were just laid on top, *with nothing to hold them down*...I'm amazed they lasted so long.'

More gasps.

'In fact, the three houses were built by unskilled workers, using bad materials, without any regard for Building Standards or Public Safety.

'I understand the Three Little Pigs have built three new houses.

'*Are they any better?* I insist they be inspected *at once*!

'I have also advised my client, Mr Wolfe, that he is entitled to sue for Wrongful Arrest, Defamation, and Damages due to being hit by a slate from a faulty roof.'

★

I haven't seen the Three Little Pigs since. I don't know whether I'll sue them or not. Getting struck off the Castle Invitation List may be enough grief for them.

I passed by Wolf Haven the other day. Empty. The Wolf Rescue League has fled though it is still possible to contact them at wwwdot.

But in another part of the country, they defended some poor sod who was sent to jail for more years than he'll care to remember. They're now getting up huge protest marches and say they'll care for him when – and if – he ever gets out.

Boy, was I lucky!

PS. My favourite bird is now the blackbird.

Elephants – easy reading for new readers who have moved on a stage. Still with –
Large type
Mostly short words
Short sentences
Lots of illustrations
And fun!

There are now five 'Elephants'
1. *The True Story of the Three Little Pigs and the Big Bad Wolf*
2. *The Hungry Horse*
3. *The Trial of the Big Bad Wolf*
4. *Jitters in the Jungle*
5. *Return of the Big Bad Wolf*

Liam Farrell lives in Maynooth, Co Kildare. This is his third 'Big Bad Wolf' story.

Terry Myler has illustrated all the **'Elephants'.** She has also written *Drawing Made Easy*.